Little Albatross

Michael Morpurgo
Illustrated by Michael Foreman

Picture Corgi

The last snows of winter were melting away.
Still, so still sat Mother Albatross, looking out
over a grey-green sea.

Underneath her, snug in the warmth of her feathers,
Little Albatross slept. He was only a few hours old,
and already strong with life.

Far out at sea Father Albatross soared above the waves, his great wide wings beating his way homewards. And he was full of the fish he had caught.

"Welcome home!" cried Mother Albatross, proud as a mother always is.

Still in his dreams Little Albatross smelt fish for the first time.

"Feed me, Father," he begged. "Feed me."

"That's what we're here for," said Father Albatross.

Little Albatross ate all he could, and then slept again.

After that, Mother and Father took it in turns. One would
go off fishing while the other stayed behind on the nest
keeping Little Albatross warm, keeping him safe.

Day by day, well fed, well guarded and warm, Little Albatross
grew ever bigger, stronger, noisier, hungrier. Through the softness
of his down he was growing fine white feathers.
And now his wings were long and wide and wonderful.

But not far away skulked a killer bird, always watchful, always waiting, and always still, so still they did not even know he was there.

Then one bright day Mother
and Father Albatross looked
at Little Albatross and saw
how big he was, and how
strong. It would be quite safe,
they thought, to leave him
for a while and go off fishing
together.

So away they flew, out over
the cliff top, singing again
their soaring song, the
song of the wandering
albatross.

They did not see the killer
bird beneath them. But the
killer bird saw them.
He was watching.
He was waiting.

"Oh Father! Oh Mother!"
cried Little Albatross,
who had never before
been left on his own.
"Come back! Come back!"

But the wind screamed
and the waves roared, and
they could not hear him.
Out over the surging sea
they soared, always on the
look-out for silver flashing
fish swimming below
them in the surging sea.
One glimpse was all they
needed.

Down they dived, deep down into the grey-green sea, hunting after fish. Then up they came again, riding the waves and swallowing all they had caught.

That night, Little Albatross slept alone on his nest. He did not see the killer bird skulking closer, closer.

When morning came,
Father and Mother
Albatross were still
wandering the ocean
together, still soaring high
above the grey-green sea,
when they saw a fishing
boat beneath them.
And look! Following
behind were thousands
upon thousands of silver
flashing fish.
A feast of fish!

Down they dived at once,
without ever thinking,
down into the surging sea,
where they snatched up
fish after fish after fish.
Then up they swam, up
towards the light, up
towards the air.

But they did not know that the fishing nets were closing in around them. They could not see them, until they swam right into them and were at once caught up, held fast and trapped. How they fought to free themselves. How they struggled.

But the more they fought and struggled, the more entangled they became.

They were helpless now in the nets, and they were not alone.

All around them they saw not only thousands of struggling fish, but dolphins were caught up too, and turtles as well.

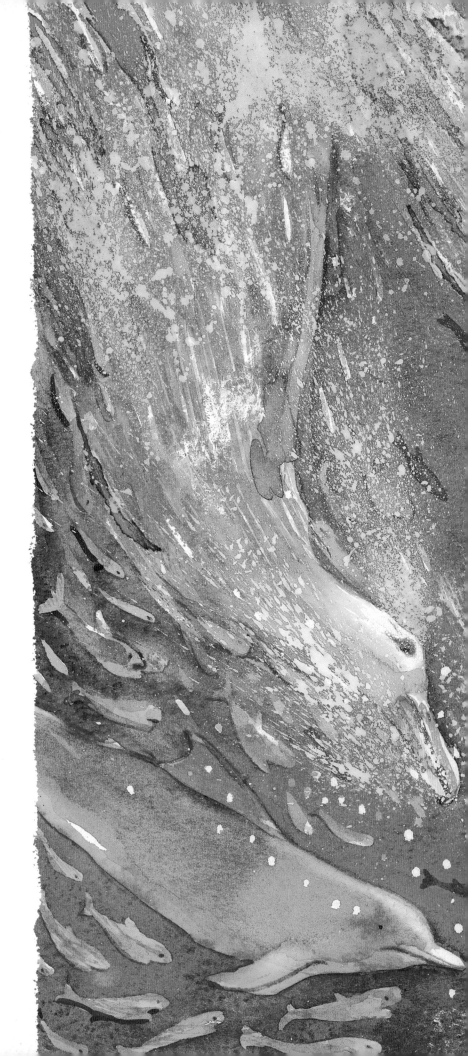

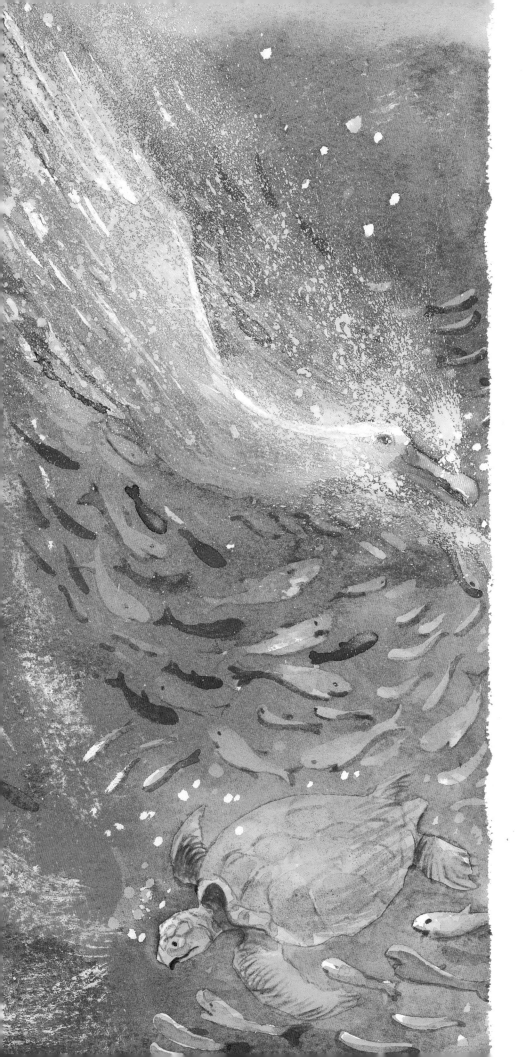

Meanwhile . . .

Back on the cliff top, the
killer bird skulked ever
closer. Closer.

And still Little Albatross
had not seen him.

Father Albatross and Mother Albatross hung in the nets, still living, but only just. When they saw the grey shark-shadow coming up out of the depths of the ocean, they made one last bid to break free.

In his greed and in his rage, the shark attacked the nets, tearing them with terrible force.

But he was too late,
for the fishermen were
already winding in their
nets. Up and out of the
sea came the nets, filled
with thousands upon
thousands of fish.

And caught up in them
were all the turtles and
dolphins, and Mother
Albatross and Father
Albatross too.

As soon as the fishermen
saw them, they freed them
from the nets. They could
see at once that the birds
were too tired to fly off. So
the fishermen let them rest.

They looked after them,
and fed them to make them
strong again. By the time
they flew off that evening,
the whole crew was there
to wave them off.

By now the killer bird was circling. He was moving in for the kill. He had waited long enough.

Little Albatross saw him coming, and saw the killer glint in his eye.

"Oh Mother! Oh Father!" he cried. "Help me! Help me!"

Suddenly, from high above them came a chilling cry. Out of the sky came Mother Albatross and Father Albatross, like two great white arrows aimed at the killer bird's heart. He knew it would be death to stay, and flew off at once.

Far out to sea they chased him and harried him until they were quite sure he would never come back.

By the time they returned Little Albatross was leaping up and down, frantic to see them, frantic for his food. But he was cross too.

"Oh Father! Oh Mother!" he cried. "I've been waiting for you for so long. I've been so frightened, so hungry. Where were you? What kept you?"

"It's a long story," said
Father Albatross.
"We won't leave you again,"
said Mother Albatross.
"Promise."
"Feed me, Father! Feed
me, Mother," cried Little
Albatross.

"That's what we're here
for," said Mother Albatross.
And they both fed Little
Albatross until he had eaten
himself happy.

Then he slept. And as he slept the first snows of winter came falling all about them. And the sound of their song floated out over the grey-green sea, the song of the wandering albatross.

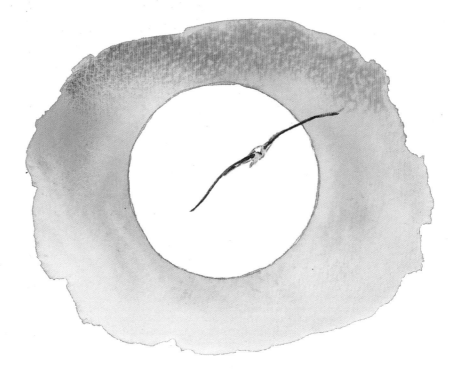

LITTLE ALBATROSS
A PICTURE CORGI BOOK 978 0 552 54698 0

First published in Great Britain by Doubleday
an imprint of Random House Children's Publishers UK
A Random House Group Company

Doubleday edition published 2004
Picture Corgi edition published 2006
This Picture Corgi edition published 2013

1 3 5 7 9 10 8 6 4 2

Picture Corgi Books are published by Random House Children's Publishers UK,
61–63 Uxbridge Road, London W5 5SA

www.**randomhousechildrens**.co.uk
www.**randomhouse**.co.uk

Addresses for companies within The Random House Group Limited can be found at: www.randomhouse.co.uk/offices.htm

THE RANDOM HOUSE GROUP Limited Reg. No. 954009

A CIP catalogue record for this book is available from the British Library.

Printed and bound in China

The Random House Group Limited supports the Forest Stewardship Council® (FSC®), the leading international forest
certification organization. Our books carrying the FSC label are printed on FSC®-certified paper. FSC is the only forest
certification scheme endorsed by the leading environmental organizations, including Greenpeace.
Our paper procurement policy can be found at www.randomhouse.co.uk/environment.